MAGICAL COLLEGE

.

Episode 16**

.

NEXT MORNING***

.

Snow won't get up from bed and Elena has been trying to cheer her up
"Snow, one boy rejection isn't the end of the world please don't do this to yourself" Elena said softly
"I've loved him for so so long very long I can't count, is it my fault to fall in love so badly for him!, I'm so in love with him that I can't even think straight but he told me he don't love me Elle, he said we are not meant to be" Snow cried even more
"Snow please you didn't sleep a wink last night, if you continue like this then you might get sick" Selene joined in while Ruby is just sitting on the chair with an angry expression
It got to a point that Ruby couldn't take it anymore then she stood up angrily
"That's it, I'm going to Daniel and I'm breaking all his bones" she said angrily and made to leave
"Woah woah woah" Elena stood up and blocked her way
"You can't do that, it's not his fault" she said
"It's not his fault?? Or are you just defending him cause he's your friend!" Rubby snapped angrily
"Well yeah he's my friend and Snow is my friend also but I think Daniel did the right thing by letting her down now instead of lying to her and hurting her feelings later" Elena reasoned
"You-
"She's right Ruby, it's not Daniel fault love isn't by force anyways" Snow interrupted, still sniffing
Ruby scoffed and sat down back
"I'll get you something to eat wait here" Selene said as she wore her white huge teddy bear flip-flops
"Just get for all of us, I'll be having pancakes" Ruby pipped in, bringing out cash
"I'll also have pancakes" Elena said
"I'm not hungry" Snow muttered
"Just get her anything" Elena secretly whispered

.

SCHOOL CAFETERIA***
Selene walked tiredly to the counter where Chippy was busy attending to other students, it then got to her
"Hey baby girl, what can I get you" Chippy smiled
"I'll take two no three pancakes and one mushroom soup to go" Selene said politely
"Oh add four bottles of milk, make the last in extreme hotter" she added, Chippy nodded instantly
Chippy has super memory and can handle up to hundred orders at once without forgetting
"Can you add four bottles of water please" that was Blake who just entered, dressed in a sport outfit and is sweating like he just finished his morning workouts
"Blake" Selene smiled
He looked at her and returned it back
"How was your night?" He asked
"Well… Not to good, Snow isn't feeling well" she replied
"Oh, how is she now?" He asked
"Worst" Selene sighed
Blake wanted to say something but Chippy brought their order
"Thanks Chippy" Selene packed them
"I'll see you later Blake" she smiled at Blake who just pinched her cheek cutely in response
One Selene way out, she bumped into Ariana who gave her a very scary look before walking past her
Selene sighed of relief, this her intimidating sister if hers!, Before leaving the cafeteria

Blake went to the field were his friends were sitting

"The bottle water?" Lan asked, painting heavily

"Here, don't die" Blake chuckled and gave him one, he threw for Daniel and Raphael and have his too

They were chatting but Daniel has been silent through out

"Bro what's wrong, you've been quite it's unlike you" Lan said worriedly, Daniel only just looked at him and sighed

"Tell us what's bothering you, girlfriend left you" Raphael mocked

"Get serious Raph" Blake snapped

"Guys it's nothing, ion just feel like talking today that's all" Daniel said

"Okay then , yeah I met Selene earlier and she told me that Snow is sick, since last night" Blake said

"What??" Lan shouted while Daniel just looked elsewhere and inhaled hard

"What kind of sickness?" Lan asked

"Ion know" Blake replied

"That's sad, that cute thing" Raphael shook his head

"I guess I caused it, I'm really sorry Snow but I can't do this to my friend, he has liked you for so long now" Daniel thought looking at Lan who had a worried expression on his face

.

SOME HOURS LATER***

They just finished having their class, Snow is on her way to her hostel when Lan came chasing her from behind

"Snow just a minute please" he pleaded, she paused and turned to him

"I heard you're not feeling well so I brought you drugs and also some food" he said handing a nylon to her

"Ion need it, I'm fine" she rejected it, without stretching her hands

"Please Snow, just have this please" he pleaded desperately

"I said I'm fine" she snapped and left him

"Just notice me for once, it's all I ask" he thought, staring at her back sadly

Daniel was watching from far and sighed, he came to rub his shoulders, giving him a weak smile

"If he knows the girl he loves, likes me instead how would he feel" Daniel thought sadly

"The nerve of him" Ruby cursed, looking at Daniel angrily

"Leave him and let's go" Selene took Ruby's hand but she slapped it off immediately and walked out

"She acts tough but she has good heart" Selene thought, she scanned for Elena and found her with Dexton as usual

***

.

Ruby is angrily practicing her sword skill in the garden, no matter how bitter she is if there's one thing she doesn't joke with then it's her friends

She still remember the first day, she came here when her father would warn her not to make friends or smile, the main reason is coming here and being the best and one-day to be a great warrior that de.mons would tremble at her sight alone

She avoided Elena and Snow like plague but they never give up on her, she chases them with bitterness but they smoothes her up like butter, they treated her like human unlike her father

Her thought was disturbed when she heard footsteps approaching her, you don't need to tell her who that is, that's the person that's always annoying her, when the footstep got closer, she angrily threw the sword at the person.

.

MAGICAL COLLEGE

.

Episode 17

.

The sword slashed Raphael's hand even when he tried dodging
"What are you doing here?" Ruby asked angrily
"Must you be bitter everytime, by the way I came to check out the garden" he shurgged and then looked at his bleeding arm and it began to heal immediately
"This garden is mine, womanizers are not allowed" she said through ganished teeth
Raphael suddenly looked left and right. "I didn't see any sign that says that" he shurgged
Angrily Ruby rushed to him and grabbed his collar
"Cool down, why must you behave like a wild animal all the time, I hope you know you're a lady" he said dryly and unfazed with the angry looks she's giving him
"Wild animal??" She said in anger, holding his collar even tighter
"Yunno ion just wanna hit you,we both know you're no match for me so respect yourself" he smirked
Ruby smiled and pushed him hard, making him land on his butt
"Apart from that what other talent do you have?" She asked and stretched her hand towards her sword, making it appear on her hand
Raphael stood up and moved closer to her
"I also know how to melt a bitter person" he said but what he felt next was slight pain
Ruby just digged her sword deep into his stomach, the sword is not poisoned so it can't kill him
"Hope we never cross paths ever" she said and then withdrew and left
Raphael hold his bleeding stomach and it healed immediately
"Really" he smiled bitting his lips

.

Dexton and Elena were eating together at the cafeteria
"So any plans for today?" He asked
"I'm planning on keeping my friend company, she's sick" she replied and took from his beef then shoved it into her mouth
"Can't your other friends do that, it's Saturday and I wanna spend it with you" he said, caressing her cheeks
"As much as I'd love to but no please understand" she said cutely
"Fine but please stay a little longer, what will I look at if you go with them" he said se.ductively making her blush
Ruby just entered the cafeteria looking angry as usual, she went straight to the table were Elena and her boyfriend where eating and banged her hands on the table, startling them
"Elena! Don't tell me you're bailing on us cause of him" she said angrily
"Who are you calling him, I'm her boyfriend" Dexton said angrily but Ruby paid him no attention
"Let's go" Ruby said and grabbed Elena's hand to leave but Dexton stood up and held her hand
Ruby looked at his hand on hers in anger
"How dare you" she gritted her teeth and slapped him hard on the cheek
Elena gasped and stood up in awe
"Let's go, can't you see this pest is just distracting you!!!!" Ruby said angrily
"He's not a pest, he's my boyfriend" Elena yelled
"Boyfriend my rump, let's go" Ruby said angrily but Elena sat down
"I've decided to spend the whole Saturday with my boyfriend, do your worst" Elena said stubbornly

"Stand up" Ruby ordered
"Make me"
Ruby just smirked and nodded
"Don't say I didn't warn you" she said before leaving
"Geez it's too much for her" Elena said angrily, using her hands to fan herself
"Ion think she likes me" Dexton pouted
"Pay her no attention, she don't like anyone" Elena huffed
"She's so in love with him now look her friends are beginning to suffer, what a loser" Mabel laughed from afar where her and her crew were watching and eating at the same time
"The great Elena is crazy over a guy, how worthless" Ariana laughed too, but then her eyes cought Blake who was just passing by through the window
"Excuse" she stood up and rushed out
****

.

"Blake" Ariana called he looked at her and smiled and began coming towards her
"He's coming" Ariana thought, bitting her lips and arranging her hair se.ductively but then he walked passed her
She gasped and turned back only to see him hugging Selene, they were holding hands and saying somethings and what annoyed her most was they way they were smiling at eachother
"Only me get to smile at him like that, it's not fair" she thought angrily, she watched them till they were out of sight
"What an epic fail" Daniel came laughing from behind
"Why are you stalking me!" She snapped
"Stalking you?? You wish" he smirked and walked past her but paused after a few steps
"Stop being obsessed with Blake and your sister, it doesn't suit you" he added before leaving completely
"Wrench" she cur$ed at him

.

Snow is sitting alone on a swing, trying to calm herself down, she has been crying nonstop, no matter how much she tries to control it
"Calm down Snow, he's not the only guy in this school crying won't solve anything" her inner self scolded her
Daniel and Lan are hiding at a corner of the school park and watching her
"Dan I can't watch this, just help me do one thing give her this medicine cause she won't even collect it from me" Lan said
"What make you think she'll collect it from me?" Daniel asked
"Cause I know, just go" Lan replied in a pleading state
Daniel sighed, he took the medicine and appeared to her
"Snow" he called
She looked at him and inhale hard
"Just wanna say you shouldn't work yourself up to much cause of what I said, I'm sorry for breaking your heart and I hope we can still be friends" he said but she didn't reply
"Here, it relive pains and headache probably heartache, just have it" he handed it to her and she slowly collected it
Lan felt a sting in his chest, he has seen the way she looks at Daniel everytime and how she behaves when she's with him, how hyper she gets when she sees him around
"Small world isn't it" he thought painfully, Daniel appeared back to him looking somehow
"Told you she'll take it from you, tell me what did you tell her?" Lan asked
"I. Well, she.

"It's fine Daniel you don't need to hide it, I've seen how she looks at you it's obvious she likes you, just tell me the truth already?" Lan said

"I'm sorry, she said she likes me and I turned her down" Daniel said lowly

"I thought as much" Lan smiled painfully before disappearing

Daniel sighed and left the place too, he bumped into Elena on his way out

"Please no questions" he groaned

"You know I'm gonna ask" she said, before grabbing his ear and disappearing off

***

.

They were now in the school spot

"Why?" She asked

"Why what?" He asked back

"Don't play with me Daniel" she snapped

"Oh I'm bad just cause I turned a girl down?" He said sarcastically when Elena gave him a look and he sighed

"My friend Lan, has loved that girl for so long and now she told me she likes me what did you expect me to do or to feel" he said sincerely

Elena looked at him and sighed, she knows very well what his saying is the truth

"But you don't like her right?" She asked

"No I don't" he shook his head and Elena sighed again

"We are better off as friends and-

"Shut up PJ, I've heard enough" she cut him off with a playful look

Daniel gasped long and hard

"You did not just call me that??, You know very well that I hate that name" He said but she stick her tongue out to him and ran off

"Hey wait, I still need a lot of advise from you" he yelled and ran after her

"I'll answer you only if you can catch me" she stopped and smirked

"Elena I'm..

"Bye" she smiled and began running again

"I'm tired" he groaned and ran after her

"Exercising is good, Incase if don't know, if I first you to my hostel forget about the advise" she said firmly still running

"Fine" he yelled and began running after her tiredly.

MAGICAL COLLEGE

.

Episode 18

.

Daniel finally cought up with Elena
"What's it PJ" she asked
"Stop calling me that!" He groaned
"What? PJ?" She teased
She was doing it purposely, she knows very well that Daniel hates that name his mom tried giving him, everytime he's mom and dad would fight over it but thank goodness his mom has forgotten all about it
"We agreed that you'll never bring this up, how can you be bullying me like this I-
"You'll tell Aunt Emma" Elena interrupted
"You, I hate you" he grumbled
"And I love you baby bro" she ruffled his hair with a smile
"But on a serious note what should I do?" He asked
"Just call her and tell her the reason why you can't date her" Elena said and Daniel nodded
"But are you sure you don't like her?" Elena asked
"I don't, geez you're just like your mother. Good night" without waiting for Elena's reaction he disappeared
"Stubborn goat" she scoffed before finding her way to her hostel

.

ROOM 180***
"Why are you late" Ruby asked the moment Elena stepped in
"Are you my mother to question me like that" Elena fired back
Selene stood up from the bed and moved to them
"You guys please don't start…" she tried talking
"Back off" Ruby yelled
"Don't yell at her" Elena yelled at Ruby too
"Elena you used to be a serious student but now you're just a fool, you're following that guy that'll do you no good" Ruby said
"That guy is my boyfriend, we love each other and I think you're just jealous because you'll never find one, because all the guys are scared of you and won't see you as a girl, because you're to mean, because.."
Elena stopped when she noticed she was getting out of control, they both stood in silence for a while before Ruby spoke
"I hope you won't regret defending that loser one day" she said before leaving
Selene looked at Elena somehow while Elena had a regretful look on her face
"I'll be in the bathroom" she muttered and slowly went there while Selene could only sigh and go out to check on Ruby

.

Ruby is sitting on the large chair outside, the words Elena said to her kept ringing all over and over
Of course she wanna be jovial, she wanna be active like other girls, she don't want people scared of her or calling her a boy but all this would only make her weak

She still remembered when a de.mon wiped away her family,her mother gone and she was separated from her twin brother and worst part was that, there was nothing they could do about it

After that her father changed, he turned icily cold and changed from her father to her mentor, he trained her almost everyday not sparing her a day to rest, he would advise her not to make friends or mostly never fall in love, cause they are all weakness

Not only that, he made her swallow a detachment pill, detachment pill is like a spider web that blocks the heart to people and mostly falling in love, that's why Ruby most avoid all they guys she knows like plague, she most treat them coldly in other for it to remain sealed

Her thought was interrupted when Selene came to join her in the sit

"What,now?" She asked coldly

"I know you're worried about Elena and want the best for her but don't blame her, you're also at fault maybe nextime try sounding sweet and not harsh then things won't turn out lik-

Selene didn't get you finish when Ruby grabbed her by the throat

"Are you asking for an early grave?!" She threatened

"No but I just want you to know that you're a good person, acting tough and scaring people doesn't suit you" Selene managed to speak

"You don't know me, this is who I am mind yourself" Ruby said before releasing her and angrily going to the room

"My neck" Selene pouted cutely, rubbing her neck

.

MONDAY**

TRAINING GROUND**

"Front, back, side, other side, jump. Good job" master Morris said to the students he was teaching sword practice

"Good news, few of you guys would be selected for a journey to the Underworld as a stage two of why we are here, they'll be an upcoming text next month, people who pass would be going while people who loose would have to stay here so one word is be prepared cause it's gonna be tough" master Morris said

"Yes master" they all bowed

"Y'all are dismissed" he ordered before disappearing

"Cool, I can't wait to go to the Underworld, do you know you'll get to wear cute robes" Snow said happily

"Ion like it there, I prefer wearing my trousers" Ruby said dryly

"Of course, you don't like anything" Elena said with an eye roll

"And I wasn't talking to you!" Ruby snapped

"You guys, stop you are not babies anymore" Selene groaned out of frustration and left them

Elena glared at Ruby too before leaving

"I need to talk to her, I'll fix what I broke" Daniel said from where he was

"She likes you, just date her if it will make her happy" Lan interrupted

"I can't do that, what about your feelings" Daniel said

"Well.. if she's happy..then-

"Just stop! Don't hurt yourself I'll be back" Daniel said and then went to Snow

"What do you want now?" Ruby asked, feeling annoyed and glaring at him

"I just need to talk to Snow" Daniel replied

"Well she doesn't wanna talk with you, stupid heart breaker now get lost" Ruby hissed out loud

"This girl" Raphael murmured from behind

"I'm sorry" Daniel muttered before using his magnetic force to pull Snow closer and disappearing real quick

"S¢um!" Ruby yelled angrily

"Is she always bitter?" Raphael asked so loudly so she'll hear but she just shot him a dangerous glare before leaving

"I'll go find Selene" Blake said and left too

.

****

Daniel appeared at the school fountain with Snow

"Let's sit" he said and she nodded. They both sat down in silence

"Look Daniel it's really cool you don't like me so-

"I'm really sorry Snow, it'll be selfish for me to love you, my friend Lan has liked you for so long now and I can't do that to him" Daniel cut her off, he said it so fast that he was even holding his breath and when he was done, he released them

"So my own feelings doesn't matter?" Snow asked with teary eyes

"It's not like that, it's complicated and I can only just say I'm sorry" he said

"It's fine, please just stop I'm trying to move on, don't remind me of this ever again" Snow said before she disappeared

"At least I tried my best" Daniel grumble

"Blake" Ariana shouted from behind, when she saw Blake walking at the front of her in the school compound

"What" he paused and faced her

"Just wanted to ask, if we could study together for this-

"I'm sorry, I already have partner" he cut her off

"Selene?" She asked in a well controlled anger

"Yeah, I'm sorry" he smiled and left her sight

Tears were threatening to pure from Ariana's eyes as she had her fist clenched tight

"Selene" she said between gritted teeth.

.

MAGICAL COLLEGE

.

Episode 19

.

Blake and Selene spent hours studying together at the library together, Selene kept stealing glances at Blake who looked focused with what he was reading
She purposely yawned loud to catch his attention but no, he kept reading looking as serious as ever
"Blake come on, we've been studying for hours already" Selene groaned loudly
"And you're crying?" He asked not taking his eyes away from his book
"Why won't I cry, I haven't eaten yet, I'm starved like hell" she grumbled like a child
Blake closed his book and looked at her, he chanted something and an apple with a little fruit box appeared on her desk
"How am I sure this is real" she scoffed
"Cause I bought it and kept it for you, yunno Incase if this happens. Now eat up" he ordered
"But-
"No excuses Selene, eat up so we can resume reading" he hushed her
Having no choice, Selene sighed and started munching on the juicy apple
"Mental note, don't ever study with Blake ever again" she said inwardly
Finally she was done done eating and as promised, they resumed their reading

.

One hour later***
"Blake" Selene called again, he stared at her tiredly
"What's wrong this time?" He asked
"I'm tired, we've been studying for 7 hours straight you are going to kill me" she complained
"10 hours is too small, what are you a baby?" He asked feeling amused
"Well, fine let's quiz ourselves and we'll call it a day?" She asked
"You're just lazy, but I'll accept" he smiled and faced her probably
About half an hour they were done quizzing themselves
"You did great" Blake smiled and high fived her
"Yeah" she smiled and stood up
"Let's hang out Blake, we've been here for hours how about we go to our reading spot and go play?" She asked
"You wanna swim there don't you?" he asked with a chuckled
"And play with flowers, and dance and shout and also drench you with water" she laughed
Blake looked at the silly cute thing, in front of him and could only just shake his head
"Let's go" he smiled
"Yeeye!" She screamed and pounced on him in the twink of an eye, they were already there

.

Selene won't stop screaming and running everywhere, she would cut some flowers and throw it at Blake who was just laughing
"Woooooooooooo" she kept on screaming and running
"Calm down Selene" Blake muttered
"No way, this is to fun" she stretched her hands to the water, allowing then to splash on Blake
He gasped and looked at her feeling flabbergasted while she sticked her tongue out at him
"Oh you wanna play, fine then let's play" he began chasing her around

Selene kept laughing and running but it got to a particular place that she stopped.
"What's wrong?" Blake asked
"Blake" she called, moving a bit front. "Something is here" she said as she knelt on the ground and began knocking a spot
"Come on Selene, get up and-
He didn't get to finish cause the ground suddenly opened and took her in
"Selene!" He screamed
***

Master Morris is sitting in his chamber and meditating but his eyes suddenly flew wide open
"Amora" he muttered

.
SCHOOL CAFETERIA**
"Dexton pay attention" Elena complained for the umpeeth time
They were trying to study but he kept pressing his phone
"Dexton" she yelled this time and he finally looked up
"You're not even paying attention" she said
"I'm sorry babe but I need to rush, I'll study with you later bye" without waiting for her reply or reaction, he pecked her forehead and ran off
Elena sat there, looking stupefied, Ruby smirked from where she was before standing up and going to meet Elena
"I won't be surprised if he breaks your heart"
"Must you always be bad omen" Elena replied with a glare, before facing her work
****

.
Master Morris appeared to the special spot where Blake and Selene do study, he was shocked to see Blake rumming about with a panic expression
"Blake" master Morris called slowly
"Master" Blake turned to him and bowed immediately
"What are you doing here, how dare you come here!" He yelled furiously
Blake was just silent
"Who else is here with you?" Master Morris asked, taking close steps to Blake
"Selene, the ground.." Blake didn't even know how to explain
"Impossible" master Morris muttered to himself

.
Selene hissed in pain and looked up. "what is this place" she thought
The place looked like a caven, everywhere was dark and shinning with blue crystals everywhere like a decoration
Looking a bit front you'll see a throne and a water fountain like the school own except this one is extremely blue and shinning also there was a blue shining swimming pool at a corner
"The full moon pool" Selene muttered, she have read about this pool in a book, for those water spirit that posses fish tales only
Selene moved around till she saw a crystal Cascade placed on an ice desk. "Huh?" Was only what could come out of her mouth as she moved closer
Now she can see a woman that has a long silver hair, lying flat on her back, dressed in a fancy princess robe
"Is she dead or is she sleeping" Selene thought

From the way you can see things, her skin looked really smooth and she has this extreme beauty that almost tempted Selene to feel
As if she was hypnotized, Selene brought her hand to the crystal and immediately it started shining some blue lights
"What the- she couldn't finish what she was saying cause she was seeing things she don't really understand
A woman with a long silver hair, fighting multitude of people and in her second hand she's carrying a baby, the rain the lighten strike the clashing of the swords was unbearable for Selene
She can see a baby falling off a cliff now. "Arghhhh" Selene screamed and hold her head tight
Master Morris appeared there, he did some finger formation that separated Selene from the Cascade
"Master" Selene could only just bit her lips as she bowed
"How did you get here?" Master Morris asked
"I don't know?" She replied lowly
Master Morris chanted somethings that made vanished Selene out of the caven, he then looked at the woman sleeping in the Cascade
"Amora" he muttered lowly.

.

MAGICAL COLLEGE
.
Episode 20
.
Selene appeared outside the caven and met Blake staring at her with a worried expression
"Selene" he rushed to her and hugged her really tight, inhaling her scent
"Selene are you okay,did you get hurt, what happened down there?" He asked all at once
"I'm fine, trust me" she smiled and cupped his cheeks lightly
"Just be careful please, now tell me what happened down there?" He asked
Selene is about to tell him when master Morris appeared to them
"Master" they bowed
"Listen, this is the last time you two will ever step foot here, understood" he said firmly
"Yes master" they bowed
"You may leave" he said and they nodded
Blake hold Selene's hand and they both teleported out

.
SCHOOL CAFETERIA***
Blake and Selene appeared to the cafeteria, they both ordered drink and sat together
"So will you tell me what happened down there?" He asked again
"I saw a woman who has long silver hair, seems like she was sleeping inside a crystal Cascade"
Selene shurgged, drinking on her fruit juice with a straw
"Wait, a woman? Silver hair, that must be the legendary water goddess Amora" Blake said
"Water goddess?" Selene asked confusedly
"You don't know her story, she once rule this place 18 years back but then it was attacked by
de.mons and that time water goddess Amora gave birth to a bouncing baby girl, she fought with
multitudes of de.mons alone" Blake said
"What about her husband?" Selene asked getting interested in the topic
"Unfortunately he died when she was in labour" Blake answered
"What?? How?" Selene asked, bitting her lips this time
"Before water goddess Amora got pregnant there was a war between, their clan and tyrant de.mon
clan, she was $tabbed five times and was at the verge of death but king Drucula used his will to save
her"
"He placed his hands on her chest and cried out, he begged the heavens to take his life in exchange
for hers and yes, the request was answered. Water goddess Amora woke up but king Drucula life
span was shortened that's why he died" Blake answered
"But how did, water goddess Amora fell asleep?" Selene asked again
"She was cur$ed, she fought with multitudes of demons, even their demon master Cyflus, but before
Cyflus died he summoned a Flyan" Blake paused and smiled
"I know you'll ask what Flyan's are so I'll tell you. Flyan's exist hundreds of years ago, they are like
fairies but they grant only one wish after that one wish they die, one thing is that Flyan's are very
hard to find they were seven in numbers and six were used by our ancestors"
"Luckily Cyflus found the last one, before he died when water goddess Amora stabbed him, he
summoned his and made his wish which is… He trailed off

"Come on!" Selene yelled

"Which is water goddess Amora would fall asleep forever until, her daughters blood touches her but then the demons would feel free to rampage anyhow they want, during the fight with the demons, Cyflus slashed goddess Amora hand which made her baby fall of a cliff, the curse took immediate effect, goddess Amora fell asleep for 18 years now and her daughter never showed up, guess she's dead" Blake narrated

"How did you know this, I've never read a book like this" Selene asked

"I guess I do read more than you" Blake replied

"Wow" Selene shook her head

"So tell me was she pretty?" Blake asked

"She was more than pretty, her long silver hair was tempting to touch" Selene replied before standing up and stretching her body

"I'm tired, I donno how many hours I spent listening to your story" she yawned

"Okay then we'll call it a day, it looks like we'll study in the library from now on" he said, standing up too

"Yea" Selene chuckled

"Good night" he moved to hug her and pecked her forehead which made her blush

"Good night" she smiled shyly before waving at him and leaving

.

A MONTH TIME: TRAINING GROUND**

Master Morris stood at the front of the whole students with a long paper on his hand

"So today would be team work and this team work would be related to the Underworld exam. I'll be calling a boy and a girl each of you would be giving a task to do at different sections of this field"

"In each section, three red badges are hidden and you must find them but I will be sending some hybrids as an obstacle on the way, your healing powers won't work if you get injured and most importantly you must find the three batches and come out in an hour time, failure to pass won't be accompanying us to the Underworld which is starting next week" master Morris said

Little murmurs could be heard

"Listen carefully, I'll pick you and your paternal and I'll be calling the names just once" master Morris said before starting

"Ruby and Raphael"

"Snow and Lan"

"Elena and Dexton"

"Selene and Blake"

"Mabel and Kenny"

"Daniel and Ariana"

"Lyla and Jason"

And some others students more…

They stepped out and their section was given to them, Ariana won't stop looking at Blake and Selene's direction

.

It pained her a lot that she was not paired up with Blake but that jerk Daniel who paid her no attention as he entered the section given to them

"Now we'll know those that will start stage two with us" master Morris said to some other mini authoritatives of the magical academy.

.

MAGICAL COLLEGE

.

Episode 21

.

Ruby and Raphael could be seen wandering about in their own section, actually Raphael has been talking non-stop but Ruby paid him no attention
"So I woke up and found myself on someone's bed, I was tied up and damn, earth girls are crazy can you believ-

.

"Dmn! Shut up for once" Ruby snapped
"I get that you're boring and I'm just trying to make this event fun for bo-
"Shhh" she hushed him by hitting her sword on his chest sharply
"Look, it's a badge" she said
"Yeah let's go get it" Raphael smiled, he made to move front but she held him back
"Finders keepers loser stay outta this" she said firmly
"Fine" he rolled his eyes
Ruby is about taking it when a hybrid jumped to attack her, she fought that one effortlessly but four more came
Raphael just stood there smirking and folding his arm on his chest, watching how the almighty tomboy was struggling to fight with over ten hybrids
"Raphael you stupid cow, a little help" she exclaimed in annoyance, slashing every hybrids coming to her
"Finders fix it yourself, losers stand smile and watch" he said in a smugy way
"I can't believe this, isn't this team work" she said as she made to kick the hybrid behind her but it cought her leg and flipped her over, making her fall
"This is hilarious" Raphael laughed while Ruby glared at him from the floor
"Okay fine" he smiled and brought out a bow with six arrows with his powers, he aimed them at the hybrids and fired
The arrows cought them straight and they all vanished to smoke
"All done" he smiled, the bow disappeared from his hands
"Help me up please" she said nicely
Raphael gave her a suspicious look but still came to her, he stretched down his hand to help her stand but she pulled him down, sat on his stomach and pinning his ne¢k
"You're such a fool yunno, now where's the badge?" She asked, fuming with anger
"First of all, what you're doing to me is inappropriate, secondly the badge is with me" he showed her
Earlier while she was fighting he had took it
"Oh" she exclaimed and immediately stood up from him, she bit her lips and looked elsewhere
Raphael stood up and smiled, looking at her side view
"Ruby you're pretty, a little smile on that cute face of yours won't harm" he said
Ruby turned to look at him and their eyes met for a while suddenly she hissed in pain when she felt something ache her heart
"What's wrong?" He asked in concern but she just pushed him away and began walking front
"Always acting tough I see" he smiled silently

.

Snow and Lan were silent throughout, Lan was thinking of how he'll start a conversation while Snow was angry with him

To her it's Lan fault that Daniel couldn't love her back, maybe if Lan haven't liked her then there might be a chance with Daniel

Snow eyes cought the badge hanging at a very long tree, she made to move front but Lan grabbed her back by the forearm

"Remember master Morris sent assassin so anything can go wrong" Lan said worriedly

Snow gave him a hateful look and yanked her hands off him. "Don't ever touch me!" She warned

"Okay I'm sorry, I get you're vexing but don't transfer it on me cause it's not my fault" he said

"It's your fault if you haven't liked me then there might be a chance with Daniel but no, look what you've cur$ed, it's all your fault" she yelled out tears with that her tiny cute voice

All what she said hurt Lan deeply, tears nearly fell from his eyes but he hold it back with his strength

"Is it my fault I like you, is it my fault that my heartbeats for only you, is it my fault that I can't stop it or is it my fault for loving you" he yelled too

Snow looked at him and said nothing expect tears pouring from her eyes

"I hate you" she cried

"Fine then, loving you was my mistake, I'm sorry" he said in a broke voice and then moved forward to where the badge was hanging

One hybrid is running towards him but he just slashed it with his sword immediately, he stretched his hands to the red badge and it appeared to his hand, Snow turned opposite direction and cleaned her tears before leaving to find other badges

.

Elena kept fighting with various size of hybrids with her long rope, Dexton is down again when a giant hybrid slashed him with it's nails

"Come on Dex, you can't afford to give up now at this point" Elena yelled still fighting, whipping any hybrids coming to her with her rope

By now Elena has found two badges and it was remaining one, Dexton managed to stand up while holding his bleeding stomach

"Look, it's up in that hill, go get it I'll take care of this hybrids" Dexton said

"But you're stomach.."

"I'm fine go" he hushed her, she looked at him and nodded before running, using her rope to slash every hybrids coming to her direction

Dexton watched how she climbed the big rock. "She's amazing" he thought

.

"Ion know why you have to be my partner, why can't it be Blake" Ariana kept complaining but Daniel ignored her completely

"I wonder what Blake is doing with Selene now, those two seems so close and it's annoying, why won't-

"Stop being useless missy, you haven't done anything other than complaining. These two badges I've found was all me you didn't help!, Every second Blake this Blake that! Get over that stupid obsession" Daniel snapped

"You. How dare you" she made to hit him but he cought her fist and pushed her back

"Just thirty minutes more, let me find that badge so I can leave you to die here!" Ariana said through gritted teeth

She turned to live but two giant hybrids appeared at her front, blocking her view, she gasped and summoned her sword to fight them but it slashed her leg with it's long nails and with a push it send her flying back

Daniel saw the scene, he rushed to the hybrids that were times ten bigger and taller than him and began attacking them

Ariana struggled to stand but her legs failed are injured badly and her healing powers couldn't work, turning to her left she saw the last badge lying on the ground just few steps away from her Ariana smiled to herself. "Let's see who's useless now" she began crawling over to it, just two steps to it, the ground began sinking

Daniel just took down the hybrids, he turned to Ariana and his eyes widened

"Please help me" Ariana cried trying to stop herself from sinking, Daniel rushed over to her, he grabbed her wrist immediately before she could sink

"Please save me, don't let me fall" she pleaded

"If you don't wanna die here then shut it" Daniel said and closed his eyes, he dragged her up with all his strength and in this case his hand got badly injured

He pulled her out successfully and then used his powers to take the badge, Ariana lay on the floor panting heavily while Daniel stood up

"Let's go" he said and started moving forward, he turned to look at Ariana who was struggling to stand

He moved to her and bent down. "Hop in" he said

"W. What?" She stuttered

"I said hop in, I'll carry you and come on no time" he reminded

Slowly Ariana climbed his back, she bit her lips hard with all what was happening now, she could hear him wincing a bit because of his injured arm

"Thank you" she didn't want to but found herself saying it for the first time in her life

Daniel didn't respond, he just wish time will fly fast and all this would end
.

Blake just finished attacking the hybrids while Selene rushed to him from no where

"Look, I found the last badge" she smiled

"Awesome" he smiled and hugged her tight before pulling away and cupping her cheeks

"For your reward?" He said

"What?" She asked and he smiled as he pecked her nose and cheeks

"Not fair" she blushed slightly while rubbing on the spot

"Let's go before we fail" he said, taking her hand, she looked at him and nodded before they both ran out

*****

.

Outside**

Elena is the first to come out, holding Dexton who's injured

"Master" she smiled, showing master Morris the three red badges

Ruby and Raphael came out next they handed their badges, Blake and Selene came out third Snow and Lan came out forth, Mabel came out fifth and her partner couldn't make it, it was remaining one more person and it was five minutes to go

"Daniel is not here" Elena said worriedly

"Daniel come on man, you can do this" Lan prayed silently

30 seconds more. No one

10 seconds more. No one
Seconds were counting faster but slowly Daniel came out with Ariana at his back who looked embarrassed
Huge smiles appeared on their faces especially Elena's
"Let's clap, we've made it" Raphael shouted and they all started clapping expect from Ruby who just folded her arms on her chest.

.

MAGICAL COLLEGE
.
Episode 21
.
Ruby and Raphael could be seen wandering about in their own section, actually Raphael has been talking non-stop but Ruby paid him no attention
"So I woke up and found myself on someone's bed, I was tied up and damn, earth girls are crazy can you believ-
.
"Dmn! Shut up for once" Ruby snapped
"I get that you're boring and I'm just trying to make this event fun for bo-
"Shhh" she hushed him by hitting her sword on his chest sharply
"Look, it's a badge" she said
"Yeah let's go get it" Raphael smiled, he made to move front but she held him back
"Finders keepers loser stay outta this" she said firmly
"Fine" he rolled his eyes
Ruby is about taking it when a hybrid jumped to attack her, she fought that one effortlessly but four more came
Raphael just stood there smirking and folding his arm on his chest, watching how the almighty tomboy was struggling to fight with over ten hybrids
"Raphael you stupid cow, a little help" she exclaimed in annoyance, slashing every hybrids coming to her
"Finders fix it yourself, losers stand smile and watch" he said in a smugy way
"I can't believe this, isn't this team work" she said as she made to kick the hybrid behind her but it cought her leg and flipped her over, making her fall
"This is hilarious" Raphael laughed while Ruby glared at him from the floor
"Okay fine" he smiled and brought out a bow with six arrows with his powers, he aimed them at the hybrids and fired
The arrows cought them straight and they all vanished to smoke
"All done" he smiled, the bow disappeared from his hands
"Help me up please" she said nicely
Raphael gave her a suspicious look but still came to her, he stretched down his hand to help her stand but she pulled him down, sat on his stomach and pinning his ne¢k
"You're such a fool yunno, now where's the badge?" She asked, fuming with anger
"First of all, what you're doing to me is inappropriate, secondly the badge is with me" he showed her
Earlier while she was fighting he had took it
"Oh" she exclaimed and immediately stood up from him, she bit her lips and looked elsewhere
Raphael stood up and smiled, looking at her side view
"Ruby you're pretty, a little smile on that cute face of yours won't harm" he said

Ruby turned to look at him and their eyes met for a while suddenly she hissed in pain when she felt something ache her heart
"What's wrong?" He asked in concern but she just pushed him away and began walking front
"Always acting tough I see" he smiled silently

.

Snow and Lan were silent throughout, Lan was thinking of how he'll start a conversation while Snow was angry with him
To her it's Lan fault that Daniel couldn't love her back, maybe if Lan haven't liked her then there might be a chance with Daniel
Snow eyes cought the badge hanging at a very long tree, she made to move front but Lan grabbed her back by the forearm
"Remember master Morris sent assassin so anything can go wrong" Lan said worriedly
Snow gave him a hateful look and yanked her hands off him. "Don't ever touch me!" She warned
"Okay I'm sorry, I get you're vexing but don't transfer it on me cause it's not my fault" he said
"It's your fault if you haven't liked me then there might be a chance with Daniel but no, look what you've cur$ed, it's all your fault" she yelled out tears with that her tiny cute voice
All what she said hurt Lan deeply, tears nearly fell from his eyes but he hold it back with his strength
"Is it my fault I like you, is it my fault that my heartbeats for only you, is it my fault that I can't stop it or is it my fault for loving you" he yelled too
Snow looked at him and said nothing expect tears pouring from her eyes
"I hate you" she cried
"Fine then, loving you was my mistake, I'm sorry" he said in a broke voice and then moved forward to where the badge was hanging
One hybrid is running towards him but he just slashed it with his sword immediately, he stretched his hands to the red badge and it appeared to his hand, Snow turned opposite direction and cleaned her tears before leaving to find other badges

.

Elena kept fighting with various size of hybrids with her long rope, Dexton is down again when a giant hybrid slashed him with it's nails
"Come on Dex, you can't afford to give up now at this point" Elena yelled still fighting, whipping any hybrids coming to her with her rope
By now Elena has found two badges and it was remaining one, Dexton managed to stand up while holding his bIeeding stomach
"Look, it's up in that hill, go get it I'll take care of this hybrids" Dexton said
"But you're stomach.."
"I'm fine go" he hushed her, she looked at him and nodded before running, using her rope to slash every hybrids coming to her direction
Dexton watched how she climbed the big rock. "She's amazing" he thought

.

"Ion know why you have to be my partner, why can't it be Blake" Ariana kept complaining but Daniel ignored her completely
"I wonder what Blake is doing with Selene now, those two seems so close and it's annoying, why won't-

"Stop being useless missy, you haven't done anything other than complaining. These two badges I've found was all me you didn't help!, Every second Blake this Blake that! Get over that stupid obsession" Daniel snapped

"You. How dare you" she made to hit him but he cought her fist and pushed her back

"Just thirty minutes more, let me find that badge so I can leave you to die here!" Ariana said through gritted teeth

She turned to live but two giant hybrids appeared at her front, blocking her view, she gasped and summoned her sword to fight them but it slashed her leg with it's long nails and with a push it send her flying back

Daniel saw the scene, he rushed to the hybrids that were times ten bigger and taller than him and began attacking them

Ariana struggled to stand but her legs failed are injured badly and her healing powers couldn't work, turning to her left she saw the last badge lying on the ground just few steps away from her Ariana smiled to herself. "Let's see who's useless now" she began crawling over to it, just two steps to it, the ground began sinking

Daniel just took down the hybrids, he turned to Ariana and his eyes widened

"Please help me" Ariana cried trying to stop herself from sinking, Daniel rushed over to her, he grabbed her wrist immediately before she could sink

"Please save me, don't let me fall" she pleaded

"If you don't wanna die here then shut it" Daniel said and closed his eyes, he dragged her up with all his strength and in this case his hand got badly injured

He pulled her out successfully and then used his powers to take the badge, Ariana lay on the floor panting heavily while Daniel stood up

"Let's go" he said and started moving forward, he turned to look at Ariana who was struggling to stand

He moved to her and bent down. "Hop in" he said

"W. What?" She stuttered

"I said hop in, I'll carry you and come on no time" he reminded

Slowly Ariana climbed his back, she bit her lips hard with all what was happening now, she could hear him wincing a bit because of his injured arm

"Thank you" she didn't want to but found herself saying it for the first time in her life

Daniel didn't respond, he just wish time will fly fast and all this would end

.

Blake just finished attacking the hybrids while Selene rushed to him from no where

"Look, I found the last badge" she smiled

"Awesome" he smiled and hugged her tight before pulling away and cupping her cheeks

"For your reward?" He said

"What?" She asked and he smiled as he pecked her nose and cheeks

"Not fair" she blushed slightly while rubbing on the spot

"Let's go before we fail" he said, taking her hand, she looked at him and nodded before they both ran out

*****

.

Outside**

Elena is the first to come out, holding Dexton who's injured

"Master" she smiled, showing master Morris the three red badges

Ruby and Raphael came out next they handed their badges, Blake and Selene came out third Snow and Lan came out forth, Mabel came out fifth and her partner couldn't make it, it was remaining one more person and it was five minutes to go

"Daniel is not here" Elena said worriedly

"Daniel come on man, you can do this" Lan prayed silently

30 seconds more. No one

10 seconds more. No one

Seconds were counting faster but slowly Daniel came out with Ariana at his back who looked embarrassed

Huge smiles appeared on their faces especially Elena's

"Let's clap, we've made it" Raphael shouted and they all started clapping expect from Ruby who just folded her arms on her chest.

.

MAGICAL COLLEGE
.
Episode 24
.

Ruby could hear the thumping of her heartbeat and at the same time, pains, she could feel unbearable pains
Unable to take this anymore she kneeled his balls hard
"Ouch Ruby I'm- she held her chest tight and ran off
"Ruby" Raphael yelled, he wanted to follow her but one a second thought, he stayed back
"Gosh what's up with you lately" he scolded himself, tugging his lips hard and ruffled his hair
***

.
Ruby ran to a corner and held unto the walls tightly, she began sweating profusely and then vomited blood from her mouth
"You must not fall in love"
"You'll never fall in love"
"Love are for weaklings"
Her father's word still echoed in her ears

.
The girls decided to take a walk around before they leave for the Underworld, Selene is smiling and having a good stroll around
"I'll miss you garden"
"I'll miss you compound"
"I'll miss you training filed"
"I'll miss you school fountain"
"I'll miss you cafeteria" she smiled and Inhaled
He mind driffted to that forbidden garden, one last look at the sleeping water goddess wouldn't hurt right?!
She thought and was about turning to the direction when a strong arm pulled her back
"Who are.. Blake??" She seems dazzled
"Don't tell me you're planning on going there" Blake said, actually he was talking a walk around to and bumped into little cutie
"Blake I" she bits her lips
"You'll get us into trouble Selene, let's get out of here" Blake pulled her back
"I just wanted to see her one last time" Selene grumbled with a cute pout
"You can't, it's dangerous she's actually desperate to see her daughter at all cost so if you go there she'll suck your blood dry and eventually kill you, that's why master Morris and master Vendrum had ordered us to stay away; cause she had killed a lot of students" Blake said
"Fine" Selene scowled and turned to leave
"Let's take a walk around together?" Blake asked
She pouted but still nodded anyways, they began walking till they reached a place that looks crowded
"What's going on?" Selene asked
"A party, I guess let's go" he grabbed her hands and pulled her closer

.
Raphael and Lan were sitting at the party and drinking when Daniel walked in with a cute smile
"Well if it isn't mummy's boy" Raphael smirked and Lan laughed
"Is that jealousy I'm smelling" Daniel mocked with a smile and sat to take his own drink
"We aren't gonna sit here all they right, let's look for something fun to do" Daniel said
"Sure" Raphael smiled

Elena just entered with Snow

"Look over there it's Selene and Blake, where's Ruby" Elena asked

"Ion know, mind you that she doesn't like anything fun?" Snow said

"Yeah, oh Dexton is waving at me, gotta go" Elena smiled

"So I'll be alone" Snow said feeling sad already

"I'm sorry" Elena let out a cute smile and ran off

A guy went to the front with a mic

"A little game tonight it's called dancing with the blind fold" he said and the people cheered

"So the blind folds will be placed here and you guys would cover your eyes, the guys stand over there, girls there. Once you guys have covered your eyes then the guys pick your dance partner don't spoil the fun go go" the guy said

"Let's go" Blake smiled, pulling Selene along

Ruby who has been leaning by the wall and watching suddenly sighed

"A little fun won't hurt" she thought as she went to take hers

Everyone had already tied their blind fold by now

"Now in three two one, pick your partners go go go" the guy urged

Guys were running to grab any girl their hands touched, the soft tone of the piano started playing and they began dancing

"Who am I dancing it?" Blake asked sounding unsure, in his mind hoping it's Selene

"Blake" that was Selene's voice

"Selene?, Awesome it's seems like heaven want us together" he said happily, he couldn't hide his excitement to be precised

He then pulled her close making her gasp in shock

"You're such a good dancer" he whispered in her ears, making all the hairs in her body stand and sending shivers down her spine

She was not use to his closeness

"Thank you" she managed to speak

"Selene" he called

"Hmm"

"I've been thinking of how I'll tell you this but I don't know how, I guess now is my chance" he paused and breathed

"I like you Selene, very much" he said

Selene was taken back, yes she do feel something but don't exactly know what it is plus she's also scared to get into another relationship

"I-

"You don't have to give me an answer now, trust me I'll wait" he cut her off

Selene just smiled and rested her head on his chest, enjoying the moment while it last

"Thank you" she said softly

"For?"

"For liking me, I'm flattered" she smiled

.

"Whoever I'm dancing with, you're great" Daniel said but the girl didn't respond

"This is the best night of my life" he said spun her around, allowing her back to meet with his chest

She gasped a little, feeling his hot breath on her neck

"Who is this guy and why am I feeling this way?" She thought

"Whoever I'm standing with should just shut it and don't talk" Ruby on the other hand ordered

"Yes.. ma'am" her partner stuttered in fear

.

"Who am I dancing with please?" Snow asked

"I won't tell you" the guy replied
"Please"
"No"
"Please"
"Fine guess" he said
"Daniel" she said brightly
"Seriously?"
"Blake" she sounded unsure
"For real??"
"Oh, Raphael" she said brightly
"Dude" the guy snapped
"Who are you?" She asked
"It's Lan" he frowned
"Lan?!" Snow chocked on her breath
Elena is dancing with Dexton while Raphael is dancing with some girl
"Okay times up, now for the big final, the guy removes the girl blind folds and kss the girl" the guy said
Selene heart started beating fast when Blake removed her blind folds and leaned to her
"Calm down it's just a game" he said
Selene smiled and closed her eyes, waiting for it and it came, his lips met hers. It felt so soft that she don't want it to end anytime soon, ofcourse this isn't Selene first kss but it felt so good
He kept on pulling her closely to himself while she attacked his soft hair, each of them never getting tired
Daniel removed the blind folds from his partner and was shocked to see Ariana who looks embarrassed
"Ari. Ar.." he didn't even know what to say
"Just get it over with, it's just a game" she said
"You're right, it's just a game and nothing more" he shurrged
Ariana felt something sting her heart when he said that but decides to shake it off but Daniel cought her by surprise when he claimed her lips unexpectedly
It felt soft and gentle and at the same time rough, she gasped in his mouth when he went deeper
"Okay he's good" she thought and at the same time her heart kept leaping faster
Lan and Snow stared at themselves in shock
"Well will you kss me or what" Snow finally snapped
"I. Fine but don't complain when you're breathless later on" Lan said as he took in her lips
Raphael suddenly removed the blind fold from his partner hoping it's Ruby but to his surprise it's Lyla
His eyes searched for Ruby, and he saw her kssing some other guy, his chest stinged really hard
"Raph" Lyla tried pulling him close but he pushed her back and rushed out of the party
"Raphael" Lyla called in tears.

MAGICAL COLLEGE

.

Episode 25

.

It was very early in the morning, the eleven students stood in a straight line along with master Morris
"Master Vendrum will stay here to accompany you guys here till I get back" master Morris said to the other students
"We'll be moving now" he nods at master Vendrum and then closed his eyes making a finger formation and allowing a blue portal to appear
They all stepped in one by one and Lyla won't stop crying watching her friends especially Raphael leave
Master Morris turned to nod at them again before the portal closed

.

UNDERWORLD***
It took them some hours to arrive through the portal, the area was a bit crowdy abd filled with shops
"What is this place?" Mabel asked
"Any why is almost everyone dressed in rope?" Ruby added
"The rope looks cute" Snow gushed
"Okay calm down all of you, when we arrive at our main destination we would get you all you need" master Morris said
"Really, tell me how we are gonna travel cause I don't see cars" Ruby complained
"There's a horse shop over there, here all of you take this renminbi" master Morris handed then some money
"You'll get yourself a horse and we'll ride our way there" he said
"Cool" Elena smiled
"Ion know how to ride a horse" Dexton said lowly
"Amateur" Ruby hissed at him, he collect hers and went to the horse shop
"Where are we going to exactly?" Selene asked
"College of magic" master Morris replied
"Another college" Snow frowned
"You girls talk way to much, Mabel let's go" Ariana grabbed Mabel's hand and began moving forward
"Oops" Elena exclaimed as she used her telekinesis to make Ariana trip
Ariana was about falling but Daniel cought her, she looked up at him and remembered the hot kiss they shared yesterday her cheeks burnt and she immediately stepped away from him
"Let's go I'll lead" master Morris said and they began heading to the horse shop

.

Ruby has already gotten herself a horse and was waiting for them
"I can't ride a horse" Selene grumbled
"Then I'll ride you" Blake said from behind startling her
She remembered their intense kss and bit her lips
"Come on Selene we said my feelings for you won't affect our friendship right?" Blake said
"I'm sorry" she mumbled
"It's cool, come on" he took her hand and moved forward, as usual she would feel something she can't describe
They were all picking their horse, Ruby took a black horse, Elena picked a brown horse, Lan picked a brown horse, him and Snow would share, Mabel and Ariana picked a black horse just like Blake and Selene
Daniel and Raphael were still finding a horse

"Found one" Raphael smiled

"I want a separate horse" Daniel said

"Gosh this guy is wasting time" Ruby groaned

Daniel moved a bit front and his eyes cought a black horse with green eyes

"I've found mine" he smiled and made to touch it but a pin flew and pricked his hand

"Ouch" he winced looking left and right

"That's mine" that was a female voice

He turned like slow mo to look at her and no kidding, she was one hell of a beauty, talk about round eye, heart face shape, pout lips, cute blushed cheeks, attractive lashes, slim figure. She has them all

"That's mine" she said again, moving close to him and eyeing him

Daniel shaked his head back to reality

"I'm sorry but-

"But what? Did you pay for it?" She mocked

"Well I-

"Urgh move it" she hit him with her shoulders making him stagger

"I paid for it and it's mine" she pouted and climbed the horse

"As if you can ride it" Daniel said in a sarcastic tone

"Watch me" she smirked and wiped the horse making it neighed

The horse started warming up in that process splating dust on Daniel's body since the road was a bit dusty

"See ya Mr horseless" she winked and rode off

"What just.." he opened his mouth and looked at his mates who were laughing at him

"Just hop in" Raphael said, shaking his head

Daniel began to sulk as he walked to Raphael's horse

Ariana who is sitting at the back of Mabel felt somehow with what happened earlier

"Are you all ready?" Master Morris voice rang out

"Yes master" the shouted

"Hold tight" Blake said to Selene before starting his horse

Master Morris lead the road while they followed from behind

.

COLLEGE OF MAGIC***

The place was almost like M. Magical college expect bigger and more beautiful, the front view was decorated with beautiful flowers which helped in the scent of the place

The black horse with green eyes stopped at the back of the school and Lilith stepped down

She tied the horse one place and tiptoed to the window as if she was hiding from someone, the window was super high to her destination but that isn't a problem for her

She rolled her sleeves up and began climbing the fencish wall, finally she got to the window and stepped in, she was silently closing the window when…

"Lilith" a female voice sounded

She turned fear and sighed

"Mora" she frowned

"You're back, let's go fast" Mora whispered

"Master Xian didn't suspect my absence?" Lilith asked, rolling her sleeves down and dusting her gown

"Nope what took you so long and by the way did you get the Candy?" Mora asked

"I got the candy ofcourse but my horse broke down on my way back so I had to get a new one" Lilith said

"Cool, let's go eat it in our room, Mirabel is waiting" Mora said and the both girls rushed to the direction of their room

****

.

Master Morris horse stopped at the front of college of magic with his students
"Not bad" Elena smiled
"Everyone get down, let's go in" master Morris ordered
They all got down from their horse and followed him silently, a maid led them to the pain gate and everywhere there was the definition of beautiful
"Master Morris" a man dressed in a long rope with long dark hair called
"Master Xian" master Morris smiled
"I'm honored to have you all here, I'm seeing pretty faces" he smiled
"These are my students, they'll be staying here for the time being" master Morris said
"Welcome all of you, please come with me" he beckoned them to follow him inside and they did
Two maids opened the main door and just peeking inside, seeing some few students roaming around is like wow
"Welcome to college of magic" he smiled.

MAGICAL COLLEGE
.
Episode 26
.
Everywhere looked so rich and classy but a bit modernish, it looks so beautiful that the students won't stop moving around expect Ruby who stood one place, looking unfazed about the place
"So all of you should feel free by tommorow, you'll be introduced to the students here" master Xian said
"Okay where's our room?" Ruby asked immediately he stopped talking
Master Xian called two maid to show them their rooms
****
.
The maid taking the girls to their room got there
"Just here, are you gonna pack us all like sandin fish?" Mabel asked
"Relax ma'am the room is quite big plus they are three girls inside so it's okay for all of you"
"Three girls are inside?? If you know me, you'll know I hate people" Ruby sneered
"Don't mind her, we'll stay here thanks" Elena smiled
"Acting like she's cool" Ariana scoffed inwardly
The maid smiled and left then Ruby pushed the door open without knocking, immediately she did that three girls flew out of the bed in fear
"Who are you guys?" The cutest one among them asked
"Your new roomies" Selene replied
"Cool,come in I've been waiting for you guys, I'm Lilith and these are my friends Mora and Mirabel" Lilith introduced
"Thanks I'm Snow, she's Elena, Selene, Ruby and those two" Snow said referring those two to Mabel and Ariana
"It's nice meeting all of you, you can drop your bags here" Mora gestured them to follow her and they did
She showed them a very big wardrobe where they can keep their bags
"There's enough bed for us, plus the ventilation here is really good and I can give y'all a tour tomorrow" Lilith said
"Thanks we'll love that" Selene smiled
The third girl among them, Mirabel kept playing with her extremely long hair
"This place looks cool" Elena smiled and breath in the fresh air
"We'll you've seen nothing yet" Lilith winked
"How come you're only three in this big room?" Ruby asked
"Cause students are much as this is the last one here, oh and let me tell you some school rules you'll need to follow so you won't die " Lilith said Mirabel hit her when she said that
"Die??" Snow face turned pail
"Well as long as you follow the school rules then you're safe" Lilith said
"Which is?" Ariana asked
"Which is from 9pm no one steps out if the school gate, demons are always roaming around" Lilith answered
"Now I'm scared" Snow panicked
"Stop being a ballerina, this is why most people leave cause their scared to face the second stage of being a supernatural, If you wanna archive your dream here then I'll urge you to be strong" Mirabel said
"Ion know about her but I'm loving it here" Elena smiled and fell on the bed
"Me too" Selene smiled

Ariana won't stop looking at Lilith strangely, her face is looking familiar
.
BOY'S HOSTEL***
"Okay who will knock?" Blake asked looking at Daniel
"Don't look at me" Daniel scowled
"You guys are babies, move it" Raphael pushed pass them and opened the door
Two guys could be seen inside, one is laying on the bed and pressing his phone while the other is eating a snack
The one eating a snack eyes widened and he looked at his mate
"Ezekiel, they are here" he said
The guy pressing phone looked up at then with creased brow, from the look on his face he don't like interacting
"Hi" Lan smiled
"Hey" he nods at then and stood up, dipping his hands in his pants pocket
"Who are you guys?" He asked
"Your roomie" Dexton replied
"Oh" was all he said
"Hi guys, I didn't know you guys will arrive now, I'm Edward by the way and this jerk here is Ezekiel" the second guy introduced
"I'm Daniel"
"I'm Blake"
"Raphael"
"Call me Lan"
"I'm Dexton, Dex for short" they introduced
"Cool names" Ezekiel said
"Come on in roomies" Edward smiled at them, they entered and shot the door
.
Night***
"Run don't let them catch us" two girls could be seen running but then a black smoke passed them with full speed and they dropped dead
.
De.mons coven**
In a dark luxurious palace, maids walked in rolls with a bowl of blood to a giant room where you can see a handsome young guy sleeping on a gold fancy bed
One by one they handed they bowl to an ugly thing that posses horns, it collected it and fed the young guy
His gaze went to a giant candle that still has fire on it but the fire only reduced a tiny inch
"Dmn it's still not enough" he roared and the maids flinch
"Commander, he'll need the a royal to wake up fully, only she can break the spell" a woman with long tail said as she walked in the room
"But she's dead right, there's no royals again apart from that useless thing that is still sleeping" the man said
"She's still sleeping which means her daughter is still alive and we must find her or else our prince won't ever wake up" the woman said
"You're right Catylon, we will find her but on the mean time we must still make our prince grow, hunting continues tomorrow as usual" the ugly thing said
"Yes commander" Catylon nodded
.
NEXT DAY**

Some of the girls woke up with smiles
"Good morning, how was your night?" Lilith who's dressed already and is already brushing her hair asked
"I slept really tight" Elena smiled
"So did I" Selene smiled, stretching her body
Snow cute yawn was heard
"Good morning guys" she smiled
"I told you it's cool here" Mora smiled, sitting up the bed
"You lied" Mabel said and jumped down from the bed
"I didn't enjoy my sleep maybe because you girls were snoring to loud" Ariana jumped down to and entered the bathroom with Mabel
"Pay them no attention and tell us what's next" Elena said
"Before you talk" Ruby suddenly rose up from bed, she has been awake all this while but was reading a book
"What do we do about our cloth, ion wanna put on this traditional dress you're putting on" she said
"You don't have too, sometimes I dress in casual it doesn't mean" Mora replied
"Okay then" Ruby shurgged and lay down back
"Come on go shower, here tooth brush for all of you" Lilith made toothbrush appeared in her hands
"Thanks" Selene smiled when she collected hers
"Let's bath together?" Mirabel suggested
"Sure" Elena smiled and stood up, she raised Snow up
"I'll wait" Ruby said
"Come on Ruby we are all girls, unless you're hiding a dk" Lilith said making the whole girls bellowed into laughter
"Just thank your stars I slept well if not I could have damaged that pretty face" Ruby said
"Woah okay, I'm sorry" Lilith smiled
.
Few mins later***
Elena stood at the large mirror, admiring the traditional rope dress in her body
"It looks terrible on you" Ruby smirked
"Thanks, wait what??" Elena frowned
"Don't mind her you look cute on it" Lilith smiled
Mabel and Ariana just finished dressing and stepped out
"Don't those two like anyone?" Mora asked
"Will you mind them, thanks for the rope Lilith" Elena smiled
"I want one" Snow pouted
"Come" Mirabel pulled her to her wardrobe and gave her one of her rope
"Thanks" Snow smiled
"Selene?" Mora asked
"I'm good for now" Selene smiled
"So who's hungry?" Lilith asked
"We are" the all shouted and rushed out
.
The boys were all chatting on their way out of their room expect poker face Ezekiel
"By the way I haven't seen the girls" Raphael spoke up all of a sudden
"That's only what you know" Blake laughed
"Shut up, as if you don't miss Selene" Daniel said
"Yes I miss her" Blake smiled
"I miss my babe too" Dexton said

"Blake" a female voice called him from behind

Wait that voice, he slowly turned and a bright smile appeared on his face

"Selene" he smiled and she rushed to hug him

Elena also rush to hug Dexton

"Who are these?" Ezekiel asked

"Our friends" Blake smiled and cupped Selene cheeks, telling her something

Ezekiel looked at them, they were acting like highschool sweetheart

"Sure" he shurgged

"Hey, Lan, Raphael, Blake, Daniel" Snow rushed to them but the first person she hugged was Daniel that made Lan a little jealous

"Hey how was your night Snow?" Daniel asked

"It's cool, you have to meet my roomies" she said pointing at the girls standing from behind and smiling but his gaze went straight to Lilith and was looking at her strangely

"I'm seeing new faces" Mora smiled looking at Lan

"Yes" Lilith smiled dreamily looking at Blake

"The Blondy is the cutest" Mirabel said, specifically referring to Dexton

Ruby is getting impatient and at the same time avoiding eye contact with Raphael

Ariana on the other hand was wondering what Daniel was staring at, because from afar she could see him staring at something and it was Lilith his eyes were fixed on

"Horse girl?" He called surprisedly

"Huh?" Lilith snapped from Blake and frowned at him.

MAGICAL COLLEGE

.

Episode 27

.

"You don't recognize me? Or have I grown more handsome??" Daniel said with a sly smirk
Lilith took close steps to him that he had to move back but she kept leaning close and stopped when her face is just few inches away from his
"Okay easy you don't wanna kss a stranger do you" he said with a short laugh
"Mr horseless" she smiled
"Mr horseless" Lan started laughing
"Mr horseless?" Daniel asked
"Yes because you don't have a horseless, Mr horseless, get it" she laughed and punched him chest softly while Daniel just stared at her in awe
"Mr horseless, good one but can we leave now?" Ruby shouted from behind
"It's Elena not me" Selene defended herself from where she was standing
"Elena" Ruby called but Elena won't stop smiling with Dexton
Ruby angrily went to pull Elena by the arm
"Let her go" Dexton said
" let me go" Elena complained
"You have the guts to talk" Ruby stepped on Dexton's foot and he winced
"If she doesn't wanna go with you then leave her and quit acting like Dex is your ex" Ezekiel was the one who spoke
"Son of a-
She paused and started looking at him strangely
"What?" He asked
"You, nothing" she bit her lips and released Elena and then stormed out
"Who's that?" She thought as she left
Ariana didn't like the way Daniel and Lilith were talking so she just turned away in anger
"Let's go Mabel" she said moving front
"O-okay" Mabel confusedly followed from behind
"Hey" Snow smiled at Lan from behind
"Finally you notice me" Lan frowned
"I'm sorry let me introduce you to my cool roomies" she smiled
"She's Lilith, she's Mora and she's Mirabel" Snow said
"Sure" Lan smiled
Mora is busy looking at him, when their eyes met she quickly looked away
"I'll get going" Snow said and then rushed to Selene
"Elena let's go" Selene dragged her away from Dexton
"I'll see you around" she smiled at Blake before leaving
"My girls are going, it's bad seeing you again Mr horseless" Lilith winked at Daniel and rushed to follow the girls

"Never seen a girl as crazy as that" Daniel smiled

As the girls were going, Mirabel stylishly turned back to look at the boys and then winked at Dexton when their eyes met, startling him in that process

.

CAFETERIA***

Some students could be seen eating when the girls entered

"Where's Ruby?" Mora asked

"Don't mind her, she loves being alone" Elena replied as they walked their way to the counter

"Is that hotpot I'm seeing?" Selene asked, rubbing her eyes

"It sure is and it's very yummy, let's order for a table" Mirabel said

They ordered hotpot for a whole table and were now eating when Ruby stepped in

"Eating without me?" Ruby frowned

"Oh, we thought you love being alone" Lilith said with mouthful of spinach

"You might wanna swallow that" Mora said to Lilith

"Whatever make space" Ruby came to join them, they passed her a chopstick and she began eating

"What about those two-

"Wtches, you mean Mabel and Ariana?" Snow asked

"It's not nice to call them witches, my sister is there yunno" Selene frowned

"Sorry baby" Snow smiled

"So" Mirabel cleared her throat and looked at Elena who is eating

"That guy with you earlier, is he your boyfriend?" She asked

Ruby dropped her chopstick and stared at Mirabel

"Yea" Elena replied with a cute smile and continued eating

"Oh" was all Mirabel could say

.

Some hours later***

"The class was lit" Raphael said coming out of the classroom with the boys

"You've seen nothing yet" Edward smiled

"So what do we do next?" Blake asked

"Let's go out" Ezekiel spoke

"But where?"

"Shopping" he said

"Really" Lan frowned

"Yeah, at the local mall, they've got cool stuffs" Ezekiel shurgged

"Sure then, I need a shower first" Daniel said

"I need to tell my girlfriend I'm leaving" Dexton said and Ezekiel rolled his eyes

"I need to um..

"Shut up all of you, we'll go later today" Ezekiel rolled his eyes before leaving with Blake

.

Girls Hostel**

Lilith is applying more lipgloss on her lips, she is dressed in casual this time

"Hmm, Lilith have I ever tell you how pretty you look?" Selene asked, admiring her from the mirror

Lilith turned to face her with a smile

"No but if you want to, I'm listening"

"You have the face that can make a guy go gaga" Selene said dreamingly

"Like that cute guy you were talking to?" Lilith asked happily

"Who Blake?" Selene said

"What a cute name" Lilith smiled dreamily and looked at Selene who was staring at her somehow

"Oh sorry is he your??"

"No" Selene said
"You won't mind if I fl.irt with him right?" Lilith asked
Selene wasn't sure of how to answer, she doesn't even know if she likes him
"Free world I guess" she said lowly
"Oh I love you, thank you" Lilith stood up and rushed to hug her
****
.

Mora is coming out of the classroom, on her way out she bumped into Lan and all her books fell
"It's my fault, I wasn't looking" she apologized and bent to pick it
"Nonsense, it's my fault let me help" Lan also bent to help her pick her books, as they were both packing the books they raised their head up at the same time and their eyes met for a long while
"Here" he handed them to her and they both stood up
"Thanks I'm Mora by the way" she said stretching her hand to him
"Lan" he smiled and shook her hand, when he did that she felt a lot of sparks
"I'll see you around" he smiled and left
Mora couldn't hide her smiles, she touched her chest
"It's beating really fast, I can't believe I'm a victim of that love at first sight of a thing" she said to herself
****
.

Ruby walked to where the horses where kept, she took a deep brown horse and made to climb it but someone pulled her back
"It's mine" that was Ezekiel
"This guy again?" She thought, starting at him
"Don't being creepy" he said
"I'm not staring it's just that you look familiar, like we've met before" she said
"I've never seen you, ion know what you're talking about?" He climbed the horse and rode off
"Maybe I'm over thinking things" Ruby thought, she turn to take another horse but Raphael appeared to her
"Oh no" she screamed in her mind
"You've been avoiding me after the kss, I said I was sorry right!, Please don't be mad at me" he said moving close to her
Ruby moved back and showed him her sword
"I can kill you if you double cross, ion want to stay close with a guy who knows nothing than to get into women's p.ants, a loser and a freak" she said angrily
"What if I tell you that I'll change for you" he said seriously
Ruby just laughed and turned to walk away
"I love you Ruby,it pains me that you don't know that and it pains me that guy take my feelings for granted, it pains me that you kss other guys" he yelled
Ruby rushed to him and grabbed his thr.oat
"I dare you to say that again" she said angrily
"I said I love you, do your worst" he said again
Ruby gripped on his ne¢k tightened
"I love you Ruby, I'd die to kss those lips till they get swollen, I love you so much infact I can't take it any longer yunno the first time I kssed your lips, I couldn't get if off my mind, Ruby I only want you" Raphael said seriously
Ruby stared at him in awe, the only thing she's hearing is her lips, she's about to reply but Daniel entered with dropped jaw
"O. M. G" he exclaimed.

MAGICAL COLLEGE

.

Episode 28

.

Ruby released Raphael and turned to Daniel with a deadly look
"I swear I didn't hear anything, I was just like OMG, I found a horse" Daniel quickly lied before Ruby could pounce on him
"Daniel do I look stupid?" Ruby asked
"No why would you ask me that" Daniel found himself sweating with the deep looks Ruby was giving him
"Ruby leave Daniel out of this" Raphael said making Ruby turned to him abruptly
"His right leave me out of…
Daniel paused when Ruby gave him deadly looks
"You must be joking Raphael, there's nothing like us, I don't mingle with play boys" Ruby said
"I'm pretty sure you don't mingle with boys" Daniel thought out loud but immediately covered his mouth
"Wanna die?" Ruby asked moving to him but Raphael grabbed her back
"Please Ruby"
"Let me go, if you know me then you'll know my heart is made of solid, loving me is your mistake just give up" she yanked her hands away from his and climbed a horse
"And you" she looked at Daniel who moved back
"Fk you" she showed him her middle finger before ridding off
"Sorry men" Daniel said to Raphael
"It's not over" Raphael shook his head
"Just give up, you'll never get into her p.ants" Daniel rolled his eyes
"You think I'm trying to get into her pants?" Raphael asked with creased brow
"Well are you not" Daniel asked back
"Just get lost" Raphael hissed and walked out

.

Girls Hostel***
Mora just entered full of smiles, she met Lilith, Snow and Selene giving themselves make over
"Hey baby" Snow smiled
"Hey" Mora smiled too and fell on the bed, looking like a highschool girl that just got asked out by her crush
"I know that face" Lilith smiled
"Yeah tell us" Selene said, climbing the bed with her
"Okay I do have a crush but he's from your school, M. Magical college" Mora said
"Is it Blake?" Lilith frowned
"No his not the one but he calls himself, Lan" Mora replied
"Lan" Snow face changed immediately, Selene looked at her and she understood that look
"I don't know how it happened but when I just saw him looking cute and, damn I think it's love at first sight, I do read about it on books but who knows it's actually real" Mora smiled, blocking her face with pillow
"I need to use the restroom" Snow said and then stood up and rushed to lock herself in
"What's wrong with her" Mora asked worriedly
"It's nothing, tell us more" Selene smiled, trying not to look suspicious

.

Snow pressed her back in the wall and hold her chest tight, right now she felt somehow

She was the one who turned him down right but now it hurts seeing another person liking him, what if he suddenly returns her feelings
But why is she hurt, does she perhaps likes him now, she bit her lips really hard to stop her tears
Fk that thing they call love, she don't even understand anymore
.

A park in the school, Elena and Dexton could be seen walking around hand in hand and chatting happily but unknown to them, a pair of green jealous eyes were glued on them
"Interested in him, aren't you?" Mabel suddenly spoke starting Mirabel
"Small world, you're crushing on your friend's boyfriend" Ariana is also present
"I don't know what you two are talking about" Mirabel denied
"You know and we know it, today in class I saw how you were stealing glances at him every now and then" Mabel said
"You're obsessed or in love with him??" Ariana asked
"So what if I am, what are you two gonna do, tell on me??" Mirabel said in a challenging tone
"Tell, are we friends with those people" Mabel let out a hysterical laugh
"If you want something then chase after it, don't dull yourself" Ariana said and then pushed pass her
"Good luck" Mabel followed behind
Mirabel fist is tightly clenched already
"I won't dull myself I won't" she said, looking at Elena with so much hate
.

The boys are set to go shopping, Ezekiel had came back already and they were all waiting for Dexton
Finally Dexton is spotted with Elena, he just kssed her goodbye before coming to join them
"Must you always be with her" Ezekiel hissed
"She's my girlfriend what do you expect" Dexton shurrged
"That doesn't give you see a reason to oppress us right?" Blake scoffed
"See jealous cows" Dexton laughed
"What did you say" Ezekiel made to punch him
"Dude easy, you've got quite a temper" Lan pulled him back
"Where's Raphael?" Blake asked
"He said he's not coming" Edward shurgged
"Why? Is he sick?" Blake asked worriedly
"Yeah, love sick" Daniel laughed
"What do you mean?" Blake asked
"He got rejected, can you imagine that guy tried asking Ruby out" Daniel said and the whole guys bellowed into laughter expect Ezekiel
"What's funny is she not a woman?" Ezekiel asked
"She's a man, she's worse than men she's menish" Lan said and it led to another round of laughter
"You people are sick, grab your horse and let's go" Ezekiel huffed, climbing his horse already
.

"Finally" Lilith retorted when Elena entered the room
"She keeps oppressing us" Selene rolled her eyes at her
"I just received a text from Ruby, she said she's waiting for us at the local mall" Snow said
"She's there?" Lilith sounds surprised
"I'm not surprised, let's go" Selene said
They all made to leave but Mirabel just entered
"You where were you since?" Lilith asked
"Where are you guys going let's go together" Mirabel said, ignoring her question
"Local mall" Lilith eyed her and rushed out of the room with the girls followed then Mirabel at their back who just rolled her eyes

"The horse" they exclaimed when they didn't see any horse left
"The boys took it, how dare they" Elena flared
"We'll just teleport, no big deal" Selene said with an eye roll
"Acting like she's the best" Mirabel scoffed in her head
"We'll get back at them later" Snow huffed as she was the first person to disappear
Lilith was still very much angry but disappeared too along with the rest
MAGICAL COLLEGE: Chapter 21 – 30
LOCAL MALL**
The boys kept parading the mall when the girls entered
"Jerks" Lilith shouted
"Is she talking to us?" Daniel asked, looking at his friends
She moved to them and stood akimbo
"You guys took the horse, all of them" she complained
"So?" Ezekiel said nonchalantly
"I'll pun¢h you" she made to hit him but Selene came to pull her back
"Just let it slide" Selene whispered to her
"You guys over here" Ruby waved at them from behind
"Y'all all lucky" Lilith glared at them but smiled at Blake
"I'm angry with all of them but not with you cutie" she smiled and patted his hair while he gave her a confused look
"Shameless, aren't you?" Daniel smirked
"Let's go don't let him get to you" Selene dragged Lilith who is about to reply Daniel
*****

.
Mins of shopping..
"I love this bag" both Snow and Mora said at the same time as they made to carry one bag
"You can have it" Mora smiled
"No you can" Snow said
"Hey ladies" Lan came to them and wrapped his hands around Snow shoulder
Mora felt uncomfortable watching that so she just turned to leave
"Mora right?" Lan asked before she could move
"You two should talk, I'll continue my shopping" Snow said wriggling herself from Lan
"Oh then, wow Mora I didn't recognize you with this casual wear, you look… Like an angel in it" Lan said
Snow hand frozed in mid air as she was about taking a shoe
"Oh, thanks" Mora smiled, tugging her lips making her look more cute
"Here" Lan took a bucket hat and put in on her hair
"Woah now you look more pretty, prettier than ever" he smiled
"Oh gosh" Mora screamed inwardly, this guy would kill her with blushes today
Lan is busy chatting with Mora and forgot Snow standing there like a fool, Snow breathed heavily and left their sight immediately
Daniel is going to meet Elena but bumped into Lilith, who was clearly not watching where she was going cause of the huge hat she was putting on, her face met his chest and she pushed him back
"Mr horseless try watching would you" she hissed
"My name is not horseless its-
She cut him off by showing him her hand in the air
"Ion care, it'd probably sound ugly just like your ugly face" she said and left
"Ugly face??" Daniel muttered, rubbing his cheek

“How dare she” he thought.

MAGICAL COLLEGE
.
Episode 29
.
Still at the mall***
Selene is selecting cute ropes and also casual clothes too when she felt someone hand covered her eyes
"I know it's you Blake" she smiled
"How?" He asked
"I know your scent" she replied and removed his hand then faced him with smiles
Suddenly he pulled her close and hugged her tight
"Blake" she gasped, feeling her chest pounding real hard
"I just missed you so much, it's been long since we've hanged out" he said
"Huh? But..
"Hey Selene, in this two hair pins which one do you prefer for me too…" That was Lilith coming in with hair pins but when she saw them like that she paused and turned away
"Lilith" Selene ran after her, leaving Blake in confusion
"What?" Lilith asked and paused
"I'm sorry" Selene mumbled
"You don't have to apologize, just tell me the truth do you like him too?" Lilith asked
"I. I don't know okay, I mean he told me he loves me but I haven't given him an answer yet cause I'm not sure if what I feel" Selene replied
"Selene" Lilith pun¢hed her arm lightly
"You should have told me earlier, what I feel for Blake isn't that serious, I just like his handsome face that's all" Lilith added
"You don't like him?" Selene asked and Lilith shook her head with a smile
"Just figure out your feelings, you don't wanna keep a guy waiting" Lilith winked
"Thank you Lilith" Selene hugged her, after a while they disengaged from the hug
"So as I was saying, in this one or this one which one would suit me?" Lilith asked again, showing Selene two different hair pins
"This one" Selene pointed the larger one which as a lot if designs
"Thanks gf" Lilith smiled and left
.
Selene went back to Blake in an apologic look
"What happened earlier?" He asked
"It's nothing is just that, she thought she has a thing for you so she asked me to help you two, yunno get close but now she saw us yunno hugging and.." she sighed
"I'm sorry I'm putting a lot of pressure on you" Blake said sadly
"No you're not, she said she really don't like you that much and she said I should figure out what I feel for you ASAP" she added
"What do you feel for me?" Blake asked
"I don't know, I'm not really comfortable with boys but with you it's different,I feel so free around you and I love having you around, I'm just happy to have a friend like you in my life" she said
"Then just give it into the feeling and let me take care of you" Blake said, moving to hold her hand
"Blake I'm not innocent like other girls, will you still like me?" She asked tearing up already
Maybe it's the right time to open up her secret to him
"What do you mean?" He asked

"I. I got rapped by my own boyfriend, he took my pride as a woman and worst the whole streets in my area found out about this, can you still love me, can you move around with a woman people call whore, huh?" She asked, crying already
Blake feels confused and could only just stare at her
"Nevermind, I know the answer" she said in tears and without waiting she rushed out of the mall
Blake didn't go after, he was just processing everything she said. She got raped?? The vedio got uploaded in her dimension and her people calls her name's??
He didn't know what to think, the truth is that he's just surprised and angry at the same time, angry at that baStard that mistreated an angel like this!
.

Elena has been eyeing a sword for about two minutes, just as she was about to take it, her hand jambed with someone's hand, she looked up to see Ezekiel
"Oh sorry" they both chorused
"You can have it" Ezekiel said and she slowly nodded before taking it
"Sweet" she smiled, checking it out
"Babe come see what got" she exclaimed and rushed to Dexton
Ezekiel eyes never left her until Daniel came to tap him
"What's wrong dude?" Daniel asked
"Nothing" Ezekiel frowned
"Don't tell me you have eyes for her, she has a boyfriend plus she's my sweetheart ion want her for strong headed jerks" Daniel said
"Chill, I wasn't staring" Ezekiel eyed him
"I hope so" Daniel said before leaving
Ezekiel fist was tightly clenched, he just sighed and looked down thinking of something until someone came to wrap her hand on his shoulders
It was Ruby and she only just smirked at patted his back before leaving
"Okay maybe she's looking familiar?" Ezekiel thought, staring at her retreating figure
COLLEGE OF MAGIC**
Selene arrived in the school, she jumped down from the horse and rushed to her room, she waisted no time to fall on the bed and resumed her crying
Mabel is present in the room, she stared at Selene somehow
"What's wrong with her??, Why do I care" she scoffed and left
.
.
.
.

6 years ago
Sea dimension**
"What's wrong with you Tyson why are you looking at me like that?" Selene asked
"You're just so beautiful, I can't help myself" an older guy with the arrogant face spoke as he brought his hand to her tigh
"Tyson" Selene moved backwards
"Stop being a baby Selene, we have been dating for 2 years now and I'm tired of this your stupid saint behavior" he snapped
"We'll hang out later, I'm leaving" Selene said, she took her bag and made to leave as she was staying in his house
Tyson eyes suddenly turned blue and the whole door closed itself
"I'll have what I want today" he said and began moving towards her while she was moving back in fear

"What's wrong with you Tyson you're scaring me" she screamed and tried opening the door
"Today I'm gonna have you, no escape" he said as he pulled her close with his powers and captured her lips roughly
Selene tried fighting him but she can't, he was older and stronger and over powers her
Fast forward****
"Please Tyson"
"It hurts"
"Ahhhh, please stop"
The agony cries of Selene could be heard as her so called boyfriend kept going in her with force
He spilled his rubbish on her stomach and rolled to the other side of the be d tiredly
That day spoiled Selene's life, cause he made a tape out of it and posted it on the sea internet, that everyone from the waters will see
He used her to his friends to prove to his friends that he can sleep with her and uploaded the vedio on sea internet
But then Thana, her father saw this and became angry, yes he killed the boy but that didn't stop people from the waters to stop shaming Selene everywhere age goes including Ariana
Because of this Thana made them stop their school and moved to another part of the supernatural world where no one knows them, that's where they decided to start a new school and college
***

.

Selene eyes went deep electrical blue remembering all these, her hair were flying to her back the room was super windy
"I wish I get to kill you myself" her voice sounded really different
Footsteps could be heard coming to the direction of the girls room
"I'll kill you" Selene brought out a blue, water sword and once the door opened she rushed and was about to stab the person not caring who it was
"Selene it's me" Snow screamed fearfully.

MAGICAL COLLEGE

.

Episode 30

.

Selene blinked her eyes and immediately stepped away from Snow
"What was that?" Snow asked
"It's, ion know I'm sorry" Selene bit her lips
"If that usually happens when you get angry then try controlling your anger, cause you looked really scary" Snow said
"I'm sorry, I promise" Selene pouted
"It's fine" Snow nodded and sat on the bed
"So what's wrong, you look down plus you're back early" Selene said, sitting beside her
Snow sighed and looked at Selene
"Ion know what's wrong with me Selene, I think I'm now in love with Lan but Mora also likes him and Mora, she's my friend ion want to hurt her or anything but.." Snow bit her lips
"Easy I understand, but just follow your heart, tell him your feelings and if accept your feelings then you'll explain to Mora and if he don't turn accept fate and wait for the right person" Selene said
"Thanks" Snow hugged her tight
"Hey I'm always here to help" Selene smiled, patting her back

.

Few hours later***
Girly screams were heard coming towards the girls room and the door burst opened, all the girl that went shopping came in with their stuffs and goodies
"Selene, Snow we've been looking for you two" Elena jeered, running in
"Look I got myself a sword" she smiled
"Okay how many times will you announce that, it's annoying" Ruby huffed
"Everything annoys you" Elena scoffed
"I got us this local candy, master Xian forbid us from eating this, he said it contains alcohol, so dumb am I right" Lilith smiled, eating on the candy and staggering already
"Yeah real dumb" Selene smiled
"I got you two something" Mora said handing both Selene and Snow white nylons
"Thanks" Selene smiled when she saw a beautiful rope with hair pins
Snow opened her and found a cute head warmer and a makeup kit
"Wow thanks I love it" Snow smiled
Ruby got herself arm shield while Mirabel is trying to hide what she bought
"What did you buy?" Selene asked her
"Nothing special, just clothes" Mirabel smiled
"Let's see" Lilith grabbed the bag from her and emptied it on the bed
"You got yourself bitchy clothes?" Ruby asked
"They are not bitchy, they are cool" Mirabel frowned, packing her clothes already but Elena grabbed one
"Look this dress is extremely short and it'll expose your b**bs and your bareback" Elena said
"Gimme that! You're not my mother to question me or tell me what or not what to wear okay?" Mirabel snapped, she took her dress and put them in her wardrobe and then stormed out
"We were just looking out for her right?" Elena said
"Just leave her and let's get ready for tommorow class" Lilith said
"Yeah, thanks once again for the rope Mora" Selene smiled

"You two enjoy, I'm happy anyways" Mora smiled and went to her wardrobe to keep her things
"She's nice" Snow thought

.

NEXT DAY**
Class**
The students were all seated and listening to what the teacher was saying. Blake on the other hand kept stealing glances at Selene who is paying rapt attention
"Did she really got raped, why would anyone do that to her" he thought
But the truth is that nothing has changed one bit, he doesn't feel disgusted by her infact his feelings had gotten more stronger, to protect her to make her believe he's not like other guys and that the thing he feels for her is real
He came back to reality when the class was over
"Dude whats with you, your mind wasn't here since" Ezekiel whispered
"Nothing I'll be back" Blake replied, he stood up and followed Selene who just left the classroom
Ariana is about to leave the classroom but bumped into Daniel who was rushing in, he hit her and she almost fell but he cought her and pulled her close that their faces were just inches away
"Sorry about that" he smiled making her hear skip beats before releasing her and waking off
Ariana won't stop staring at his retreating figure and Mirabel is watching from behind with a smile on her face
"So not only I have a dirty secret" she smirked

.

"Selene wait up please" Blake shouted, running after Selene who is embarrassed to face him after yesterday
"Selene wait up please" he appeared to her front and held her hand, making her face him
"We need to talk Please"
"I.
"Please Selene just come with me" he pleaded
She slowly nodded and accepted his hand, they both appeared to the school park and sat on the swing

.

"About what you told me yesterday, I know it's not your fault and ion hate you for it, my feelings haven't changed yet it's more stronger, please don't run from me" he pleaded
"Trust me Blake, I'm not a whore like people say,I'm not a slut I really didn't know it will happen, I'm not a bad person, I swear I didn't enjoy any of it" she said tearfully
"I trust you, that guy is a bastard if I set my eyes on him, I'll kill him I swear" Blake said, wipping her tears
"I thought he loves me but I was wrong, plus he's already dead so don't bother looking for him" she said with a small smile
"I didn't know you were going through all of this, I'm sorry for rushing you but just know I'm different from that ba$tard, I'd never take you for granted. Here" he brought out a diamond bracelet
"For you" he gave her
"My bracelet" Selene gasped
"Huh?"
"It looks like the one I lost to the water demon" she said
"Oh, funny I actually gifted something like this to a girl back when I was little and-
He paused and looked at her
"You're that water girl aren't you? Why didn't I thought of that" he gestured like he had just remembered something
"So you must be that my little friend" Selene said, feeling surprised

"Small world isn't it, I thought I'll never see you again, come I wanna show you something" he stood up and took her hands
.

BOYS HOSTEL**
They both appeared to the boys hostel
"I can't be seen here, it's inappropriate" Selene said, feeling scared already
"It's fine come on" Blake took her hands and led her to his wardrobe
He opened it and brought out a sketch book and gave her, Selene opened it, it was indeed a painting of when she was nine, it is painted perfectly
"This is magnificent" Selene smiled, checking out the paintings and feeling impressed
"It's been long I've painted after my mom's death, but the very first time I saw you, I couldn't help myself" he said, bringing out another sketch book and giving hers
Selene opened it and it was a painting of her side view, smiling
"This is the pretty girl that stole my heart when I first saw her at the fire works, I thought I'll never see you again so I painted this to savour the moment"
"But then I saw you at school as a new student, heaven can't describe how much, how happy I felt or how my feelings keeps growing deeper and deeper only if you can just trust me" he said sincerely
Selene looked at him with a smile
"I didn't know what to say" she poke honestly
"Selene I'm lovestruck with you, even if I have to wait hundred years then I'll wait" he said
"Blake I- she bit her lips hard
"Just be my girlfriend, I promise we'll take things slow, please" he pleaded
"I- she nodded shyly
"Please use your words, I wanna hear it"
"Yes I wanna be your girlfriend, and I want us to take this slow" she said shyly
"Selene, thank you so much" he moved to hug her tight
"Thank you so much" he hugged her, her hands found its way to his back and hugged him too
Their body were closely pressed against eachother and Blake kept hugging her tight as they weren't close enough, each of them not wanting to let go until
The doctor burst opened and Edward entered with his jaw dropped
Blake and Selene broke the hug immediately
"Oh I'm sorry for disturbing just came to get my phone which is here" Edward said with a pleading smile and moved to carry his phone
"I'm leaving now so you two can continue and-
"Just get out" Blake cut him off
Edward nodded and started leaving
"Close the door went you're out" Blake added
Edward just nodded and closed the door as Instructed
Blake smiled and faced Selene
"So where were we?" He said without waiting he pulled her for a deep kss which she reciprocate immediately
It went on for a while before Blake pulled away from her for then to both catch their breath
"I love you" he whispered
"Thanks" she smiled
"I'll take that, for now" he smiled and pulled her close again to kss her once more
.

College lounge**
Elena is busy showing Daniel her sword she bought
"It's cool isn't it" she said when she saw that Daniel wouldn't stop drooling

"Can I borrow it to practice?" He asked

"Nope only two people in this world can touch this, it's me and myself alone" she replied with a sweet smile

"You're being unfair" Daniel huffed

"Elle" that was Lilith coming with a smile to hug her

"Baby" Elena jeered and hugged her back

"Wassup?" Elena asked

"Nothing I was just passing by and-

"Oh hi horseless" Lilith smiled when she saw Daniel

"He's not horseless he's Daniel" Elena laughed

"I'll still call him horseless" Lilith said

"Yunno what, you irk me" Daniel said to her

"Bleeeh" she sticked her tongue out at him and jogged off

Elena started giving him annoying smiles

"Don't do that, you can see how annoying she is" Daniel huffed
.

"Horseless" Elena laughed and stood up

"You won't borrow your sword?" Daniel asked

"Nooooooo" she prolonged the no and packed her things then left

"I'll still take it anyways" Daniel muttered with a sly smile.
.